Saturday, 9th

I'm on the train, on my way back from Harton to Charing Cross. Dad's playing in a jazz concert and I'm going to watch him. I thought I'd use the time to fill in my diary for last week, but the train's travelling at such speed I can hardly keep my pen on the paper. It was 10 minutes late, so maybe the driver's making up for lost time. We're rocking about on the rails, hurtling through stations that are just a blur. There's no one else in this compartment but me and this boy. He's tall and thin, about my own age with badly cut fair hair. He looks nervous. Maybe he's worried about the speed of the train. But I'm not. As long as we get to London on time I don't care. I can't wait to see Dad play — it'll be the first time since Mum died last year — and I know he's going to be terrific.

As the train rocked on Jamie heard the guard calling out, 'Tickets, please,' further down the corridor. He rooted in the pocket of his too tight jeans and felt the momentary panic he often did when meeting a stranger. He was wearing his anorak, the one that was huge and didn't make him look too overweight.

'You need more exercise,' the Head had told him.

But Jamie didn't like sport.

'Look at that paunch,' one of the pupils at Harton High had shouted at him recently.

'You're a real couch potato, Jamie,' the PE instructor had said. 'We've got to get some of that flab off this term.'

But as Jamie's reaction was to forge even more sick notes, his flab had only increased.

Checking in his anorak pocket, he at last found his ticket, glancing at the boy opposite as he did so. He was also looking worried, slapping the pockets of his denim jacket and jeans, but without any result.

For a moment their eyes met and then they both looked away again as the boy continued to search his pockets.

Jamie watched him out of the corner of his

eye, feeling increasingly tense as the guard came nearer. Then he had a strange feeling. It was as if he *had* to help him. Jamie, usually shy and quite unable to speak to strangers, felt a strong urge to intervene and the urge became a compulsion. Why on earth did he feel this way, Jamie wondered. Only last week he had spotted a mate of Dad's and had hurried across the road to avoid him. This boy didn't even look very friendly.

Suddenly the train plunged into a tunnel, still rocking wildly, and the lights in the carriage flickered and went out. Without any warning, Jamie saw in his mind's eye – or thought he saw – a fleeting image of sea and rocks and heard shouting somewhere behind him which merged into the crashing of surf and the mewing of gulls. He was suddenly terribly afraid and inexplicably out of breath.

Then sound and vision vanished abruptly as the train roared out of the tunnel into the fading light of the autumn evening and Jamie felt dazed and bewildered. Had he been hallucinating? Could he be sickening for something?

Without hesitation, amazing himself, Jamie turned to the boy and asked, 'Got a problem then?'

'What?' He sounded surly.

'Can't you find your ticket?'

'Mind your own business.' The boy stopped searching his pockets and pressed his face to the grimy window, watching the suburbs flashing past. But Jamie could still feel his fear. It was so weird. He felt as if he was watching a scary film that had him in its grip. But there was something else too – this strange, uncharacteristic urge to help a complete stranger.

'If you've lost your ticket, I've got some money.'

Jamie was amazed by what he had just said. He'd never behave like this normally. So what was he doing and why had he stepped so far out of character? And what about the image of the cliffs and the sea and the shouting. Where had that come from? Again, Jamie wondered if he was ill, genuinely ill for a change, and was about to start a cold or had picked up a virus. But he didn't feel shivery or too hot and he didn't have a headache. He only had this strange and unsettling urge and the fear he couldn't explain.

'I told you to mind your own business.' The boy whipped round. 'Just push off or shut up,' he added.

Before Jamie could reply, the guard arrived at last, frowning at them already.

'Tickets, please.'

Jamie held his out. The guard studied it for a moment, clipped it and moved on to the boy, who had suddenly closed his eyes. Never had Jamie seen such fake sleep.

'Tickets, please.'

The boy let out a rumbling snore. Did he really think the guard was going to go away, wondered Jamie.

'Tickets!' the guard bellowed, grabbing the boy's shoulder and shaking him. 'Oi – you. Wake up!'

'It's OK,' said Jamie quietly.

'What's OK?'

'He's a mate of mine. I'll pay.'

'He should have got a ticket.'

'The booking office is closed in the afternoons,' explained Jamie politely. 'We both got on at Harton.' The lie was easy. Too easy. Jamie felt confident and protective.

'So how come you've got a ticket and he hasn't?' snapped the guard suspiciously.

'My dad got mine last night.'

The boy's phony snores deepened.

The guard sighed. 'What's he want then? A single?'

'Yes,' said Jamie uneasily.

'That'll be ten pounds forty. OK?'

Jamie dug his hand into his pocket, wondering why he was just about to waste his allowance on a total stranger. The boy had obviously jumped the train. It wasn't fair. So why was he paying his fare?

Jamie handed over the money and the guard glanced down at the boy. 'Why doesn't he wake up?'

'He had a late night.'

'Not on drugs, is he?'

'Course not.'

'You'll wake him up at Charing Cross?'

'You bet,' said Jamie.

But the guard was clearly unsatisfied and grabbed the boy's shoulder again, giving him a vigorous shake.

'Yeah?' He sat up, suddenly and unexpectedly. 'What do you think you're doing? Trying to mug me, are you?'

The guard was thrown. 'You were asleep. Your friend paid your fare.'

'That's all right then, isn't it?' said the boy

with irritating smugness and closed his eyes again.

When the guard had gone, Jamie said pointedly, 'I don't know why I did that.'

'What?' The boy opened his eyes reluctantly.

'I don't know why I paid your fare.'

'Neither do I.'

Jamie felt a flash of temper. He wasn't even going to get a word of thanks. 'Don't you have any money?'

'No.'

'So you jumped the train?' Jamie was outraged, but only at the loss of his allowance. 'I'll call the guard back.'

The boy gave him a truculent look.

'It's not fair.' All his allowance gone on a stupid urge that Jamie couldn't understand or justify. Worse still, the boy couldn't even care less. 'Where are you going?'

'That's my business. I don't like nosy parkers!'

'I paid your fare.'

'I didn't ask you to. Now push off!' The boy grinned and put his feet up on the seat. 'You're a right pain, aren't you?'

'I paid your fare,' Jamie repeated doggedly, wondering what to do next. If he told his dad, he'd laugh at him. He would think he'd been a complete idiot.

'You running away?'

'That's my business,' said the boy, yawning. 'You're getting boring.'

'Get your feet off the seats, you little lout.' The guard was suddenly beside them again on his return journey.

'Isn't the train going too fast?' asked Jamie. For the second time he surprised himself. It was as if he was trying to get the boy out of trouble again, trying to distract the guard. But why?

'Driver's making up time.'

When the guard had gone, Jamie knew he had to do something. He wasn't usually aggressive and never willingly got into a fight, but the loss of his allowance to a stranger who wasn't even grateful was ridiculous. He wasn't just going to sit there and take it.

Jamie got to his feet and stood over the boy, trying to keep his balance on the wildly rocking train.

'I'm going to give you my address.'

'What for?' The boy was grinning.

'So you can send me a postal order.'

'You'll be lucky.'

'You'll do what I say.' But Jamie knew the boy would do no such thing and he felt a feeble idiot as he stood there, trying to keep his balance.

'I haven't got a bean, so sit down, fatso, before I make you.'

Just then the carriage shook and Jamie almost fell.

The boy laughed unfeelingly.

'It's all I've got.' Jamie was close to tears. 'All that money on your lousy rail fare. You've got to give it back. I'll be broke.'

'That's your bad luck. I didn't ask you for it, did I?'

'I was trying to help you out. What would have happened if you couldn't pay the guard?'

'I'd have done a runner.'

'Where?'

'Up and down the train.'

'He'd have caught you.'

'Him and whose army? So you paid. You're a sucker, aren't you?'

'I'm not moving until you give me your address,' Jamie said, sounding unconvincingly threatening. 'If you don't, I'll –'

'You'll what?' The boy was sneering at him openly now.

Suddenly Jamie felt a spurt of temper that drove him on, making him take a risk he had never taken before. Drawing back his fist, he hit the boy hard in the face.

The boy stared up at him in amazement, so shocked that he was momentarily frozen in his seat. Then he stood up and something fell out of his jeans pocket which he scrabbled to pick up. When he had shoved back what looked like a small packet, the boy came at Jamie with fists flailing, the bruise on his cheek already beginning to show.

'No one does that to me,' he yelled. Then he put his fists down and tears started in his eyes as all his aggression collapsed. 'Everyone does that to me,' he muttered.

'What do you mean?' asked Jamie, startled by the sudden change and lack of retaliation.

'Don't you get bullied at school?'

'A bit.'

'I get it all the time.'

'Who from?'

'Marcus, mostly. He's – he's older than me.'

'Why *does* he bully you?'

'I hurt his brother.'

'How?'

'We lit a fire in the wood. Henry got burnt.' The boy was talking slowly now, his face tense and strained.

'Badly burnt?' Jamie's curiosity was getting the better of his anxiety.

'It left a scar, but only a small one. Marcus has been having a go at me ever since. In the end he got his mates to chase me up this cliff and I almost fell off.'

Cliff? Jamie froze as he remembered the image that had filled his mind earlier. Had this boy planted the picture in his mind? How could he do that?

'I'm running away,' said the boy and then he smiled triumphantly. 'But I've got photographs – evidence that could get him into big trouble. *And* he knows it.'

'What evidence?'

'Enough. It'll fix him.' He pulled out a packet from his pocket and then shoved it back again.

'So why are you running away?' demanded Jamie.

'I want to make him sweat – just for a while.'

The tears filled the boy's eyes. 'But someone's got to help me,' he whispered. 'How about you?'

The carriage gave a terrific lurch and there was a banging sound from the front of the train which was followed by a screech of brakes. Fearfully, they gazed into each other's eyes.

'What's going on?' Jamie yelled as the train lurched again and the whole carriage reared up like an angry horse. There were crashing, grinding sounds, and as Jamie began to fall towards the boy he saw that one of the doors had burst open. In a few seconds he was going to be outside on the track. He flailed about, unable to regain his balance, but the boy suddenly caught him and shoved him back with surprising strength. Jamie collapsed in the opposite seat as the carriage stopped rearing, bashing the side of his head.

'Someone's got to help me,' yelled the boy again, rushing at Jamie, dragging a packet out of his pocket.

But as the carriage settled back on the track, the door that had opened slammed shut again, hurling the boy on to the floor. Crashing into a broken seat, he hit his head with a terrible thump.

The train finally came to rest and was still. A silence enveloped them like a smothering blanket.

2

Jamie could hear screams and shouts and the slamming of doors. Poking his head out of the window, feeling a surge of pain, he saw the carriage was halfway across the line at a forty-five degree angle. The screaming grew louder and he could smell smoke. Staggering to his feet, Jamie leant over the boy who had a deep wound in his head.

He took out his handkerchief and tried to staunch the blood, but it flowed straight through, soaking his hands. Leaving the handkerchief in place, Jamie peered out again. He needed help desperately, not so much for himself but for the other boy.

Several people were walking along the line, carefully avoiding the electric rail. Others were staggering around looking dazed, while a woman lay ominously still near the next carriage which was partly tipped on its side.

Jamie could see a footbridge hanging at a crazy angle above them. One of the carriages must have hit the supports which were now badly buckled, while the rest of the train lay at various angles across the track. Jamie could hear someone crying and he could still smell smoke but there was no sign of any fire.

He returned to the boy, relieved to see that the blood seemed to be slowly clotting into dark lumps. His mouth was half open and when Jamie gently took his wrist he thought he could detect a faint pulse. But he wasn't sure.

Jamie felt thoroughly confused. The boy had pushed him back into his seat just as the train had derailed. Why had he done that? Why had he instinctively helped him when he had been so ungrateful about the ticket?

Suddenly an image of cliff and rocks and sea filtered back into Jamie's mind. This time he could see every detail – the irregularities of the cliff, the different shapes and sizes of the stones on the beach and the smooth boulders at the edge of the sea as a great wave crest crashed on to the shingle in a cloud of spray. Was that how it had seemed to the boy? Jamie shivered.

Then he heard the sounds of sirens. They seemed to calm his mounting anxiety a little – an anxiety that, strangely, seemed to have nothing to do with the crash.

Jamie went to the window and peered out again, to see dozens of fire officers and paramedics moving up the line with cutting equipment and stretchers. The sight of them was incredibly reassuring.

'There's someone hurt bad in here,' he yelled out of the window. At first none of them seemed to hear him and Jamie bellowed again. 'Someone's been badly injured. You've got to come!' As one of the paramedics began to run towards him, Jamie heard a voice in his head. *Someone's got to help me. How about you? Why can't you help me? Or don't you want to?*

'The name's Joe. What's your name?' The paramedic was deliberately slow and reassuring, but Jamie only felt furiously impatient. They were wasting time. The boy could be dead.

'I'm Jamie Todd. I tried to stop the blood with my hanky.' His voice broke. He needed his mother; she'd have known what to do.

The paramedic opened the door and pulled himself up into the carriage, quickly squeezing Jamie's arm and then making his way to the boy who lay so still on the floor. Joe drew out a torch and shone a pencil beam into his eyes. 'Can you hear me?' he asked. 'Can you tell me your name?'

But the boy's eyes didn't show a flicker of life.

'Is he dead?' asked Jamie, his voice trembling, hardly able to bring out the words.

'I've got a pulse.'

'What's the matter with him?'

'He's unconscious. We're going to have to move him out fast. What about you?'

'I'm OK.'

The paramedic looked at him closely. Then he said, 'You could have concussion. You've bashed your head too, but not nearly so badly. I think you should come to hospital as well.'

Panic swept Jamie again. 'I can't – I'm meeting my dad –'

'Has he got a mobile?'

'Yes.'

'Know the number?'

'It's in my diary.'

'Let's get your friend out first and then I'll call your dad.'

'He's not my friend. I've never met him before.'

'You didn't talk to him at all?'

'A bit.'

'Know his name?'

Jamie shook his head.

Joe hurried to the door and clambered down on to the track. 'Jump,' he said. 'I'll catch you.'

Jamie obeyed and the paramedic caught him, staggering a little under his weight. Then he turned away, blowing a whistle and shouting to his colleagues.

'We've got a nasty one up here.'

For a moment, Jamie wildly imagined Joe had some secret knowledge and the boy was a well-known villain. Then he realised he was referring to his injury and a new wave of alarm washed over him as he realised how much he cared. But why *should* he care? He could feel himself hurting inside. The boy was a stranger. In Jamie's ears, however, there was a crunching of waves on a stormy beach and the sound of gulls high up in the sky. He couldn't see them, only hear their plaintive cries. Was the boy trying to share his experience with him? Or was the image just playing and replaying in his mind as a result of the bang on his head?

Jamie watched the strange boy being gently lowered from the carriage to the track by a chain of paramedics.

Once the boy was down, he was taken at a run on a stretcher towards the waiting ambulance.

'You're sure you don't know anything about him?' asked Joe, who had stayed behind.

Jamie began to explain about how he'd paid the boy's fare and how ungrateful he'd been. But when he started to tell Joe the rest of the boy's story, he felt a sudden pounding in his temples and a headache which was so bad that he could hardly bear the pain. Directly he stopped talking, however, the headache went away.

'So he might have been running away,' mused Joe. 'He didn't have a bag or anything in his pockets at all. It looks like he'd deliberately stripped away any means of identification.' He paused. 'But not quite.'

'What do you mean?' demanded Jamie

'I found a tag on his shirt. It just read Peter.'

So the boy had a name at last.

3

I'm in hospital. The train crashed...but I'm fine, well almost fine. I've got a bash on my head and I might have concussion, but I'm OK. After the crash I was in a state of shock, hardly knowing where I was, but then I saw the boy, who is apparently called Peter, lying on the floor, blood pouring from his head, and all I could think of were his last words: 'Someone's got to help me. How about you? Someone's got to help me —' What did he mean? And why should I help him after he refused to repay the ticket money. I don't know why but I feel inexplicably drawn to him. I wonder why he didn't have a bag or a wallet or any identification at all? And why didn't I tell the paramedic the full story? But I couldn't. I physically couldn't. Every time I tried, the headache became too bad. It's as if something was stopping me...but what?

I hate hospitals — I'm sure I've been feeling much worse since I arrived — I hope Dad hurries up...

Jamie lay in his hospital bed, propped up on pillows, writing his diary. He had undergone tests for concussion but he felt fine, especially now he had been told Dad was on his way. Although he had asked for news of Peter no one seemed to be able to tell him anything.

When Dad arrived Jamie was overjoyed to see him. As usual, Dad looked casually comfortable. He never seemed out of place anywhere in his old cords and crumpled sweater, his white beard looking as shaggy as ever and his kind, cornflower-blue eyes full of concern.

But Jamie also noticed how tired he looked. 'I'm sorry you had to miss the concert, Dad,' he muttered guiltily.

'It's not every day your only son gets caught up in a train crash. Besides, Bert Hanks took over. No one's going to miss me.'

Just then the doctor arrived with the staff nurse.

'We've taken a look at your scans and there

doesn't seem much wrong. But we'd like you to stay in overnight – just in case.'

'In case of what?' asked Dad.

'It's better to monitor cases like these for at least twenty-four hours – just to be on the safe side.'

'I thought you said there wasn't much wrong. Can't I take Jamie home?'

'The doctor's right,' interrupted the staff nurse. 'We don't want to run any risks.'

'I'm sure we can discharge your son before lunch tomorrow. But we do need to observe him overnight.'

Jamie looked anxious. He didn't want to spend any more time here.

'Can I be with him?' asked Dad.

'I'm sure you can. Staff Nurse will find you a bed somewhere. I'll make an appointment for his GP to see him. All he needs is a few quiet days, a lot of sleep, and then I'm sure he'll be fine.'

'That boy in my carriage,' asked Jamie hesitantly. 'Was he badly injured? His name's Peter. The paramedic found a name tag, but he didn't have anything in his pockets and he wasn't carrying –'

The doctor looked impatient. 'I'm afraid I

haven't been treating him.'

'Was anyone killed?'

'Fortunately not.' The doctor was walking hurriedly away now. 'But there were quite a few serious injuries. I'm going to check on some of them now.'

Dad picked up a newspaper and urged Jamie to try and get some sleep. But that was an impossibility. He *had* to know how Peter was. He had to find out.

'Dad –'

'Mm?'

'I can't sleep.'

'Maybe they can give you something.'

'I have to find out how Peter is.'

'You can't get out of bed.'

'*You* find out then,' Jamie insisted.

'I'm not a relative.'

'Please, Dad.'

Suddenly the strip lighting on the ceiling opposite Jamie's bed began to flicker. There was a crackling sound and it went out.

Mr Todd sighed and put down his paper and Jamie smiled at him gratefully. 'I'll go to reception and see if they know what's going on.

But they may not tell me anything.'

Dad slouched out, his favourite black boots creaking as he went down the corridor.

Jamie and his father had always been close. They shared similar musical tastes, loved old films and watched them together for hours in the living room of the Victorian house at Harton.

'You're a couple of couch potatoes,' Mum had told them repeatedly, but Jamie never minded her friendly insults for he knew, like his father did, that Mum respected the way they both 'lived in their heads', as she had put it. 'I don't know why you two bother having bodies at all. You could just be floating minds, little blobs moving about in the stratosphere.'

Jamie closed his eyes, still listening to the familiar creaking sound which gradually merged into something else that was also familiar but he couldn't immediately identify. Then Jamie realised he was listening to waves on shingle again and a spark of fear ignited. At the same time, the smaller strip of lighting on the wall behind his bed shimmered and then popped. Jamie gazed up at it in consternation. What was going on? Why had another light gone out?

Then the strip cracked from end to end and bits of plastic and metal rained down on Jamie's bed.

'This is all very odd,' said the staff nurse, bustling up. 'Don't move. I'll go and get a dustpan. This part of the hospital's only just been rewired and it's been fine until tonight. That's the second light to blow in an hour.'

As she bustled off, Jamie desperately tried to clear his mind of anxious thoughts, but instead found himself imagining he was standing on top of a cliff, looking down at a sheer drop, the waves nudging a rocky beach. A group of small birds darted in and out with the tide at the water's edge.

Behind him, Jamie heard boys shouting, but there was nowhere left to go for they were coming up on both sides of the clifftop. What was he going to do? His panic surged like the tide below and the waves seemed to be drawing him with immense power, wanting to pull him down.

Peter, yelled one of the boys. *We're coming to get you, Peter.*

'No!' screamed Jamie and opened his eyes to see the friendly face of the staff nurse who was carrying a dustpan. She looked concerned and put it down, leaning over, taking his hand.

'What's the matter, Jamie?'

'That's not my name.'

'You were thrashing about in the bed and then you began to call out. Don't worry. You've had a bad shock and got a bit confused, and what with the lights... There's another strip gone now by the door.' She began to delicately pick off the plastic and metal, dropping them into the dustpan. Jamie hardly noticed what she was doing, or what he was saying.

'I told you. Jamie's not my name. Why are you calling me Jamie? You've got mixed up. My name's Peter.' Blind panic filled him. Although he could hear himself talking he didn't seem to be in control of the words. And though he could no longer see the waves, he could still hear them.

The staff nurse patted his wrist, pulled up the blankets to his chin and tucked Jamie in so tightly that he felt trapped, suffocated. 'Would you like some Ovaltine?' she asked. 'It'll help you go off to sleep again.'

That was the last thing he wanted. Sleep meant he would be back on the clifftop again. 'Where's my dad?' Jamie demanded.

'He's gone downstairs. He won't be long. Try

and rest.' Then the staff nurse asked hesitantly, looking concerned, 'Is Peter your middle name, Jamie?'

'Peter's my only name. Can't you understand? My name's not Jamie. It's Peter.'

They stared at each other and then the staff nurse sat down and held his hand, a look of concern on her face. 'I know it's all very confusing,' she said.

'What is?'

'You've been badly shaken up and you might have concussion. You know you've been in a train crash, don't you?'

'Of course I do,' Jamie snapped. 'Do you think I'm crazy or something?'

'Of course not, you're just muddled, that's all. You're registered here as Jamie Gordon Todd. There's no mention of Peter.'

'Why should there be?' demanded Jamie. 'I'm not called Peter. That's not my name.' His head was pounding and Jamie felt dizzy.

'Of course it's not.'

'What are you on about Peter for? He's unconscious in another ward, isn't he? It's not me who's muddled.'

The staff nurse got up. 'I want you to relax.

Now why don't you accept my offer of that Ovaltine? It'll make you feel nice and sleepy.'

Just to get rid of her, Jamie agreed, and she hurried away. When she had gone he felt ashamed for she had done all she could to help him. He leant back feeling exhausted, but as he closed his eyes, an urgent voice burst into his thoughts.

Jamie, came the voice in his mind. *You've got to help me.*

4

What's happening to me? Why did I just call myself Peter? I can't get him out of my head, it's as if he's controlling my thoughts, infiltrating my dreams. And when I close my eyes I keep seeing this scary clifftop. If this is concussion then it's really weird. I feel confused and I want to go home, far away from Peter. I wish I'd never met him.

'You all right, son?' his father asked when he returned.

'I'm fine.'

'You sure?'

'Yes. What's up?'

'It's just the staff nurse told me you said your name was Peter. That's this boy's name.' He sounded agitated.

'I expect I'd been dreaming.'

Ken Todd looked relieved.

'Well?' asked Jamie impatiently. 'What did you

find out about him?'

'They just said he was "poorly".'

'What's that meant to mean?'

'I think it means they're not saying anything.'

They looked at each other, understanding there was nothing more that could be done, but Jamie still felt a wave of angry frustration. A wave? Suddenly he heard the sea again, crashing on rocks. Then the sound abruptly faded and the subdued noise of the ward returned. 'Don't they know who he is?'

'If they do, they're not saying that either.'

'Hasn't anyone come to see Peter?'

'I don't think so.'

'Where is he?'

'Winston Ward.' Ken Todd hesitated. 'Wait a minute. Don't you start getting any smart ideas about wandering round the corridors and trying to find him.'

'I wouldn't do that, Dad.'

'You would, given half a chance. Look, Jamie – you're meant to be under observation. You're not to put one foot out of bed.'

Jamie sighed – he could never hide what he was thinking from his father. Quickly he changed the subject. 'The staff nurse has gone to get me some Ovaltine. I'm going to try and get some sleep.'

'That's what I want you to do. And just in case you get any big ideas in the night I'm going to make sure the night staff know you might be getting itchy feet.'

'Dad!'

'I know you.'

Jamie grinned. 'Where are you going to be?'

'They've got me fixed up with a bed in a side ward on the second floor. OK?'

Jamie nodded and yawned, lying back on the hard pillows, his head hurting. Dad still looked at him suspiciously.

'You're not going to let me down, are you?'

'No chance.'

'OK.' He bent over and kissed Jamie on the forehead. 'Don't do anything I wouldn't do.'

Just then the staff nurse returned with the Ovaltine, and Jamie sipped it as she hurried away again. Dutifully, he closed his eyes but he had never felt so wide awake.

How seriously injured *was* Peter? Jamie had to know. Surely a nurse would be more successful at finding out the truth than his father, but he would have to find another one. Then he spotted a much younger nurse.

'Excuse me.' He sat bolt upright in bed. Glancing down at his watch, he was surprised to find the time was still not long after midnight.

'Yes?' She looked tired and overworked.

'I'm sorry to bother you, but I was in this train crash.'

'I know, love.' She was warmer now and came over and sat on the end of his bed. 'How are you feeling?'

'OK. But I'm worried about another passenger.'

'A relative?'

'No. A boy. We were in the same carriage. His name's Peter. He got hurt badly. I want to know how he is.'

'You're not to worry. I know the doctors are doing everything –'

'I won't be able to sleep,' said Jamie. 'I've *got* to know how he is.' His voice was shrill now and the patients on either side turned to glance at him disapprovingly.

The nurse rose wearily to her feet. 'I'll go and see Staff Nurse. Don't get yourself worked up.'

'Thanks. I'm really grateful.'

Jamie felt incredibly weak, and as the nurse

hurried away he heard the now familiar sound of waves crashing on a rocky shore. His eyes had been closing but he opened them fast, determinedly blinking away the clifftop and the sheer drop to the boiling sea below, his fear pounding as hard as the waves. The last place he wanted to be was back on the cliff. He *had* to stay awake. Then Jamie remembered that the cliffs could appear even if his eyes were open. He couldn't win either way.

Trying to distract his thoughts, he wondered what his father was doing. Had he gone straight to bed? Or, more likely, had he slipped out for a drink?

Sweat prickled on Jamie's brow, yet he felt icy cold inside. The sound of waves seemed to crash in his ears and his head felt as if someone was banging his skull on a rock. He could smell salty air, seaweed – and then the disinfectant smell of the ward.

'Are you awake?'

'Eh?'

'You were nodding off.' The young nurse was back.

Suddenly Jamie was wide awake, feeling guilty,

as if he had been failing in a duty. 'Did you find out anything?'

'Yes. I'm afraid he's very poorly.'

'What does that mean?'

'What it says,' she replied defensively.

'Is he going to die?'

The nurse looked away.

'Please!' Jamie decided to feign mild hysteria. It seemed to have worked last time. 'I won't be able to sleep. I'll lie awake all night and –'

'He's in a coma,' said the nurse. 'And that's *all* I can tell you –'

'Has anyone come to visit him?'

'Apparently not.'

Suddenly another piece of strip lighting overhead flickered and burst, just like Jamie's had, showering the floor with plastic. Some patients screamed, the nurse jumped and one of her colleagues ran over to the debris. The ward was much darker now and suddenly a familiar voice entered Jamie's head. *Someone's got to help me.* But how *could* he help Peter? He was in a coma.

'Isn't that a bit weird?' asked Jamie as the nurse watched her colleague clear up the mess. She was shivering slightly and shaking her head.

'I just don't understand it. The rewiring was only done recently –'

'Not that,' snapped Jamie. 'I mean the fact that no one's come to see Peter.'

'Well, we haven't been able to contact anyone. The paramedics said he'd got no identification – only a tag in his shirt with the name "Peter" on it.'

'I wondered if he was running away,' Jamie suggested hesitantly, trying to drag her attention away from the lighting problem.

She shrugged. 'The police have been, but of course they can't talk to him.'

'Do you think they'll want to talk to me?' asked Jamie.

'Not till the morning,' she replied firmly. 'You're not allowed to see anyone tonight except your dad.' The young nurse looked at him sternly and tried to be fierce. 'Now listen to me. I've told you everything I can and you've got to be satisfied, at least for the moment. It's important for you to get some rest. Are you going to try and do that for me? Despite half the lighting system blowing itself out?'

Jamie nodded and thanked her again.

*

The darkened ward was alive with suffering, and coughing and groaning punctuated what promised to be a very long night indeed – so long that Jamie began to feel afraid of lying there, unable to distract himself for hour after dreary hour.

At last he dozed off but it was a fitful sleep, and soon he was wide awake again.

He looked at his watch, dozed and then woke again to see that only five minutes had passed. He felt so hot that sweat seemed to be saturating his body. The next moment, he felt incredibly cold, as if the ward had become a refrigerator, and once again he heard Peter's voice in his head. *Someone's got to help me.* Peter began to repeat a name over and over again, but Jamie couldn't make it out. Then he heard more clearly. The name was Marcus. Wasn't that the name of the boy whose brother Peter had hurt? The boy who had bullied and chased him?

Jamie lay there, listening intently, but all he could hear now was the persistent coughing and groaning around him. He glanced across at the bed next to him and in the gloomy half-light saw a man with a long nose. He looked incredibly old and had thin strands of silvery hair flowing on to the pillow. Then he sat up – as did all the other patients. They began to chant in unison, 'Marcus. Marcus. Marcus is coming.'

'Yes,' agreed a middle-aged man a little further up the ward. 'Marcus is coming all right.'

Jamie sat up in bed, not sure whether he had been dreaming or not, utterly confused and not really knowing what he was saying. 'Peter,' he called. 'Are you there?'

Someone's got to help me –

'Where are you? I thought you were in a coma.'

Marcus is coming.

'All right, love. I'm here,' said another voice soothingly, a real voice this time.

'Who are you?'

'The name's Susie.'

The staff nurse had a bowl of cold water in her hands and a large wet cloth.

'You were just having a nasty dream. I'm going to cool you down.'

For a moment he wondered if she was going to throw the bowl of water over him. Then she gently pushed Jamie's head back against the pillow and he felt the wonderful coolness of the damp cloth.

'I'm terribly thirsty,' he pleaded. 'You couldn't

get me some *really* cold water?'

'Of course I can. I'll put some ice in a jug and you can slake your thirst.' She grinned. 'Don't drink too much, mind, or you'll be needing the toilet all night. If you *do* want to go, don't get up on your own. Push your buzzer and someone will come and help you.'

'Thanks.'

But when the staff nurse returned with the water, Jamie was flat on his back, asleep again, snoring slightly with his mouth half open, so she put the jug down on his bedside table and hurried away.

5

Jamie was lying in a small, stainless steel cell, with a highly polished ceiling which was slowly descending until he was staring up at his reflection. He had lost all sense of time and place, watching his eyes occasionally blink. Gradually his reflection became misty and insubstantial, its shape changing until Jamie realised he was no longer looking up at himself but Peter. His eyes were closed and he was hooked up to a bleeping machine, his chest rising and falling but his face lifeless, bloodless, devoid of the least expression.

Then Jamie suddenly surfaced to reality with an enormous sigh of relief. As he gazed around the slumbering ward, Jamie now knew exactly what he had to do. He sat up and pressed the buzzer.

The young nurse came over, looking exhausted.

'I need to go to the toilet.'

She nodded slowly, as if she didn't quite believe him. 'Get out of bed carefully and I'll help you.'

'I don't need any help,' Jamie said brusquely. 'I can manage on my own.'

'Do what I say,' she replied abruptly. 'And be as quick as you can because we're very short-staffed tonight.'

Not wanted to antagonise her, Jamie got out of bed and with the young nurse's arm round his waist began to make slow progress towards the toilet.

As he entered a cubicle, her bleeper sounded. 'I shan't be long,' she said, darting off. 'Another patient needs me. Don't try and get back to bed on your own. I'll fetch you in a couple of seconds.'

Jamie almost shouted aloud in triumph for she had given the him the very opportunity he wanted. Peter needed him. He had to go and find him. Faintly he saw the clifftop again and felt a stab of fear, his thoughts in confusion, thoughts that weren't always his own. Sometimes Jamie felt Peter needed him; other times he *was* Peter, needing Jamie.

He opened the toilet door, glanced round and began a stealthy run down the corridor. For the first time in his life, Jamie felt powerful and decisive. It was as if his old, fat, rather wimpish personality had disappeared. It was a strange but welcome feeling.

Eventually, Jamie saw the sign he needed. Winston Ward. Within another couple of minutes, he had arrived, conspicuous in his borrowed hospital pyjamas that were so big he had to keep hitching up the trousers.

An elderly man with a stick shuffled towards him in carpet slippers, and Jamie tentatively approached him.

'Excuse me. I'm looking for Peter, the boy who was injured in the train crash.' Jamie knew it was a long shot, for the man might have no idea who he was talking about.

But the answer Jamie needed came at once. 'Room Two. But he's in a coma. Poor little blighter.' Then he frowned. 'Are you a relative?'

'I'm his brother.'

'Shouldn't you speak to a nurse?'

'There's no need. I've already been in there. I just went to the toilet and got lost.'

The elderly man nodded and was about to shuffle on when he said, 'Were you on the train with him?'

'Yes.'

'Bit of luck *you* aren't in a coma too then.'

'That's right.'

Plucking up all his courage, Jamie pushed open the door of Room Two and went inside.

The orderly was young and well-built with curly dark hair and strong, determined features. He couldn't have been more than seventeen. He was standing next to the bed wearing a white coat, going through the pockets of Peter's jeans.

Because he looked so furtive, Jamie blurted out, 'What are you doing?'

Dropping the jeans with a start, the orderly abruptly turned round.

'What are you doing?' Jamie repeated, as they stared at each other, eyes locked.

'Trying to find out who he is.' He was stuttering slightly.

'I thought his clothes had already been checked out.'

'Do you know him?'

'Not really,' said Jamie. 'He was in the same carriage with me when the train crashed.'

'I'd better get on.' The orderly paused nervously. 'You shouldn't be wandering about, should you? You're not on this ward.'

'I came to see him.'

'You mustn't be long.' The orderly was getting agitated. 'Just a quick look. He's in a coma.'

'I know.' Jamie went over to the bed and stared down at Peter who was lying on his back, a bandage round his head, tubes running into his nose and arm, his thin face white and vacant looking. A machine hummed and Jamie could see a graph-like tracery on its screen, making bleeping sounds. Peter's hands were lying by his sides and his eyes were tightly closed. The room shimmered slightly and Jamie almost lost his balance as he had the sensation of the ceiling and the walls beginning to close in on him. Peter's voice echoed in Jamie's head and he felt sick with fear and anxiety.

'You'd better go now,' said the orderly, sounding anxious. 'A nurse will be along in a minute.'

Jamie hesitated, wanting to prolong the awkward conversation. 'Haven't they got *any* idea who he is?'

The orderly frowned. 'Come on,' he said quickly. 'There'll be trouble if you're found in here. I've got to get back on the ward. I've got another couple of hours on my shift yet.'

Just then a nurse dashed in. 'You'll have to give me a hand,' she yelled at the orderly, ignoring Jamie. 'One of the life support machines is on the blink down the corridor. Is this one working properly?' She darted over to Peter's bed and hurriedly began to check the equipment. 'It looks OK,' she said. 'Come on. I need your help.'

The orderly began to follow her, but as he went, Jamie heard the nurse say, 'I don't recognise you. Are you new here?'

'I started today,' said the orderly hesitantly. 'I don't know much about life support machines.'

The nurse laughed. 'All I want you to do is to hold a torch. Are you capable of that?'

'I think so.'

They both laughed.

Jamie went back into Peter's room and gazed down at the mysterious stranger. Despite his closed eyes Jamie felt the force of Peter's will just as strongly as he had on the train before the accident, fierce and dominating.

Jamie stood there, feeling almost possessed, as if he and Peter had been fused into one being. Somehow Peter was inside him, talking to him, controlling him, and there was nothing he could do about it.

Someone's got to help me.

'But how can I?' whispered Jamie. 'You're in a coma. How *can* I help you?'

Look after them, came the reply, strong and powerful, thrusting into his mind.

'Look after what?'

But there was no answer, and instead, Jamie felt such a rush of weakness that he could barely stand up, as if all Peter's strength had been used up.

Then a last burst of willpower snatched at him. Jamie saw the short cropped grass of a windswept clifftop, caught a glimpse of waves crashing on the beach below, heard the shouts of the boys – and then the strip lighting in the ceiling above him exploded, once again covering him in slivers of plastic.

He was shakily wiping at the debris when the door opened and another, slightly older and much more heavily-built orderly peered in.

'Can I help you?'

'I was just checking on Peter.'

'Without anyone here?' the orderly asked icily.

'There *was* someone.' Jamie was defensive. 'In a white coat. Like you.'

'An orderly?'

'I think so.'

'There *isn't* another orderly. I'm the only one on this ward.'

Jamie gazed at him, puzzled. 'He had dark, curly hair.'

'Never seen anyone like that before. Maybe he was a doctor. Now how can I help you?'

'I came to see Peter. I wanted to know how he was.'

'Are you a relative?'

'I was in the train crash with him.'

'You shouldn't be in here.'

'The other guy didn't seem to mind.'

'Look – you've got to push off now.' The orderly was impatient. 'Which ward are you on?'

But Jamie was already hurrying away, anxious not to be further identified, hitching up his tent-like pyjama trousers as he went.

The young nurse was furious when Jamie got back.

'Where have you been?' She was beside herself

with agitation. 'I told you to wait for me –'

'I'm sorry,' said Jamie. 'I must have taken the wrong corridor.'

'You've been away for over quarter of an hour –'

'I got lost.'

Just then the staff nurse appeared looking equally agitated, but Jamie soon realised her anger wasn't directed at him.

'So the wanderer's returned. Get Jamie back into bed at once, nurse. What *were* you thinking about?'

'He wanted to go to the loo and then Mr Thomas pressed his alarm and I thought he was having another attack –'

But the staff nurse was unsympathetic. 'You must never leave a patient here for observation unattended. Anything could have happened.'

'I'm sorry.' She looked so downcast that even the staff nurse took pity on her and Jamie felt very guilty.

'Just get him back into bed. And don't let Jamie go off on his travels again. You're to stay put, young man. If you need to go to the toilet again, you'll be brought a bedpan.'

Confused and still worried about the

mysterious orderly, Jamie was firmly led back to bed. Once there, he began to puzzle again over what he had felt as he leant over Peter's bed. How could someone in a coma have such strong willpower? Or had he imagined it all because he *did* have concussion or was in shock? Yet he was sure Peter had been desperately trying to reach him. Did he just want Jamie to help him out of his coma? Or was there another motive? And what had Peter meant by the words, *Look after them*, which had arrived so forcibly in Jamie's mind. Look after who?

6

Sunday, 10th

Peter's willpower is so strong I keep feeling as if I __am__ Peter. He seems really scared but I don't know what he wants me to do, and I'm as scared as he is — scared of the clifftops and the chasing boys and Marcus. Although those things don't happen to me, it feels as if now they are — I'm the one being chased up the clifftop, I'm the one Marcus is after...but perhaps it's just because Peter has such a strong hold on me... I wish Dad was sleeping in my ward, I'd feel much safer then.

Jamie paused for a moment, his eyes skimming the last entry as he relived all the events that had occurred since the train crash. As he lay there, trying to make sense of it all, he could hardly keep his eyes open, and moments later, he fell into a deep sleep, dreaming himself back into the small, shining space. This time the walls were reflecting so much blinding light that Jamie's head ached, and as he gazed up at the brightness of the ceiling, again slowly descending towards him until he could clearly see Peter's face reflected on its shiny surface, he felt an acute sense of claustrophobia and breathlessness.

Jamie woke, clutching at the sheet, his knuckles white in the semi-darkness of the ward, the sweat pouring down his forehead. He sat up, and seeing the diary and pen lying on the bed picked them up, startled to find that there was some more writing at the end – long and straggling and slanted to the right. Writing that was definitely not his own.

He flicked on the replacement light over his head and began to read and almost immediately felt breathless again.

I knew they were going to steal so I shot them with my camera. I knew they were going to steal so I shot them with my camera. I knew they were –

The sentence had been written out half a dozen times. Then it was followed by a few, even more straggling, words.

Marcus and Les made them chase me –

Jamie examined the straggling writing carefully. Looking at it again he supposed it *could* be his own. Suppose he'd fallen asleep with the diary and the biro in his hands? Or suppose he'd been only half asleep and had somehow managed to go on writing? The result would hardly be his best writing, would it?

But even if that was true, how could he describe a situation he had never experienced? Jamie stared hard at the writing. Was Peter at work again? His head began to pound and his mouth was so dry he suddenly felt desperately thirsty.

Pouring out a glass of water from his bedside jug, he glanced down at his watch. It was just after four in the morning and sleep now seemed impossible.

He blinked and in that blink saw the aluminium room with the ceiling gradually descending.

Jamie sat up and scored through the straggling writing with his biro just as the young nurse came up. She looked as exhausted as he felt.

'Awake again?'

'I told you – I can't sleep.'

She gazed down. 'You've crossed out half of your diary.'

'It wasn't right.'

'I wouldn't worry if you can't remember everything just now. It'll all come back. You shouldn't be taxing your mind like that.'

'That's why I crossed it out.' Jamie laughed, just to stop her probing.

She sat down on the edge of the bed. 'Try and relax. It's all over now.'

'What is?'

'The train crash.'

'It's not over for me.' Jamie couldn't understand why he was being so surly and rotten to her. The young nurse was only trying to comfort him.

'You still worrying about your friend?'

'He's *not* my friend.'

'The boy you met on the train then.'

'I *am* worried about him.' Jamie seized the opportunity to talk about Peter, trying to be more friendly. 'Is there any news?'

She shook her head. 'If there was, I wouldn't know.'

'You're not much help, are you?'

The young nurse sighed and got up. 'You can't

please everyone,' she said and Jamie suddenly noticed that she was close to tears.

'I'm sorry.' He felt more himself now, genuinely sorry to have hurt her. 'I'm very strong-willed,' he said, and then gave a little gasp. He hadn't meant to say that. So where had the idea come from?

Jamie remembered how Mum, speaking her mind as usual, had begged him not to have a second helping of a particularly delicious pudding, but to no avail. 'I'm only trying to help you lose weight,' she had said, and not for the first time.

'Strong-willed he wasn't, so why had he said he was?

'Have I upset you?' Jamie asked the young nurse.

She shook her head. 'I'm just having a bad night, that's all.'

'I got you into trouble.'

'Staff Nurse is always on at me. Or maybe it's because I'm always tired out. But don't let that stop you giving me a shout if you feel bad or you want anything.'

'OK.' Jamie felt guilty and deflated. He put his diary on the bedside table and tried once more to go to sleep.

Stop him!

The command was inside his head and hadn't been spoken aloud. Jamie was sure of that.

You've got to stop him.

Jamie sat up, listening intently. This time the command seemed to hover on the air, like an echo, but in reality all he could hear was the rest of the ward snoring or coughing or muttering in their sleep. The fear returned, catching at his throat, making his breathing shallow.

He could hurt me. Marcus could hurt me.

Without stopping to think what he was doing, Jamie's feet hit the floor and he began to run past the darkened beds. There was no sign of anyone official, and when he passed the nurses' station they all had their backs to him. Once out of danger, Jamie slowed down to a more reasonable pace, conscious that he was going to get the young nurse into trouble again. But he knew he couldn't help himself. He was being driven on and couldn't stop, no longer in control of his mind or his body.

Several times he tried to slow down, to clutch at the wall, to hang on to anything that would prevent him from reaching Winston Ward – and Peter.

But soon Jamie was nearing Peter's room, and when he eventually pushed open the door he was amazed to see the dark curly-haired orderly again, sitting on the edge of the bed, gazing down at Peter intently.

The machines hummed and bleeped and Jamie had the unsettling sensation that he was being strapped down. He blinked and the feeling went away.

'What do you want this time?' asked the orderly.

'What are you doing here? Again?'

'I'm just having a bit of a clear up.'

They both looked at Peter's jeans and T-shirt that were lying on the floor. Why ever was the orderly going through them again? Was he looking for something he might have missed? But was he an orderly at all? Could he be an intruder with a stolen white coat?

'Why aren't his clothes in his locker?' asked Jamie fiercely.

There was a long silence. Then Jamie's confused thoughts suddenly clicked into place. Of course. The orderly *wasn't* an orderly at all. He must be Marcus. But who *was* Marcus?

The confusion began all over again.

*

'Where did you get that white coat?' Jamie blurted out.

'What do you mean?' The orderly looked horrified, and Jamie knew it wasn't the reaction of a genuine orderly. He should have been puzzled or bewildered. 'What are you on about?' he continued. You must have got yourself some brain damage in that train crash.'

'I don't think so,' said Jamie, more confident now. 'You stole that white coat, didn't you? Where did you get it? Off someone's peg?'

'You're a right little nutter, aren't you?' The orderly was casually folding up Peter's jeans and T-shirt, ready for putting back in his locker. But Jamie saw that his hands were shaking.

'Who are you?' he demanded.

'I'm Tim Lock and I'm employed here as an –'

'Tim Lock? That's funny. I thought your name was Marcus and you were here to look for some photographs. I thought you chased Peter up to the clifftop. You and Les.'

The silence seemed to go on for ever.

'Who are you?' asked the orderly at last.

'A friend.'

Then the orderly gave a bark of agitated laughter. 'Photographs – clifftop?

'Maybe the photographs were of you stealing something.' As the words tumbled out, Jamie felt a surge of panic. Where had he got this idea from? Peter?

The orderly laughed again, but the sound was dry and hollow and on the verge of panic. Then he said, 'Get back to your ward – now!'

'No way. Shall I start shouting for help?' demanded Jamie.

'Do what you like.'

'A nurse will come.'

'Fine. You need help and she can give it to you.'

'OK.' Jamie darted over to Peter's bed and pressed the buzzer. 'Now what are you going to do?'

The orderly strode to the door and hurried out and Jamie instantly realised he'd made a serious mistake. He should have waited for him to make the first move. Now Marcus – if it was Marcus – was going to get away. What should he do? Chase after him? But it was too late. Fatally, Jamie waited as he heard brisk footsteps heading towards the door of Peter's room.

*

The nurse was middle-aged and heavily built. She gasped with surprise when she saw Jamie. 'Who are you?' she asked. 'You shouldn't be in here. What have you been doing?' She hurried across to the bed and gazed down at her patient. Then, seemingly satisfied, she turned back to Jamie. 'Who are you?' she repeated.

'I'm Jamie Todd. I was in the train crash with Peter.' He was feeling limp now, almost too tired to communicate. The fear had gone – and the frustration about Marcus's escape – but he still felt driven by a sense of urgency.

'I see,' the nurse said tersely.

'You've got to get after him –'

'Get after who?'

'There was this bloke. Said he was an orderly. But he wasn't. He was Marcus.' Jamie felt so weak, but he *had* to keep going.

'What are you talking about?'

'He'd come here to hurt Peter.'

'Our orderly wouldn't do that,' the nurse protested. 'Mick's as gentle as a –'

'He's *not* Mick. He's Marcus. He just ran out. He was searching through Peter's clothes.'

'What for?' The nurse began to back towards the door as if she was trying to get away.

'Peter took photographs,' Jamie gabbled, sure she was going to call for help. 'They show Marcus and this other bloke stealing something. Marcus wants the photos. Peter won't give them to him.'

'Who *is* Marcus?' As if rethinking what she was going to do, the nurse returned to Peter's bed.

'He was with Peter. There was this Les. He's in it too –' Jamie broke off as she pressed the buzzer.

'Which ward are you in?' the nurse asked gently, as if humouring him.

'Bartram.'

'Do you have suspected concussion?'

'No. Yes. I'm fine.' It was as if she was pigeon-holing him. The boy with concussion. Don't believe anything he says. 'You've got to get after Marcus. You've got to stop him. Marcus might come back. And if he does –'

'Why don't you sit down?'

'Where?'

'Sit in this chair. I want you to relax completely. You're not well.'

'What about Marcus?'

'This is our orderly,' said the nurse, looking at the opening door with relief. 'His name's Mick.'

Mick was massive, with a huge chest, a large head and a placid expression. It was the same orderly who had thrown Jamie out before.

'That's not him,' said Jamie.

'I thought I told you to get out,' said Mick. 'What are you doing here again?'

'Nothing,' replied Jamie.

'This boy's a patient from Bartram Ward. He's been wandering about with concussion. I don't know *what* they think they're playing at down there. Somehow he managed to find Peter. I think he knows him.'

'Of course I know him. He was on the train with me – in the crash. He hit his head.' Jamie's words were slightly slurred and his mind felt as if it was entirely composed of cottonwool.

'He's in a coma,' said the nurse firmly. 'That's why you shouldn't be in here. Peter's seriously ill.'

'Then why did you let Marcus in?' muttered Jamie.

The nurse exchanged a meaningful look with Mick and left the room.

'I want to see Peter,' said Jamie muzzily, standing up.

'He's here. You can look, but don't touch.'

Mick stood with his arms out, ready to grab him at any moment.

Jamie's thoughts were in slow motion, yet he felt as if someone was probing at them, trying to get something across to him but without success.

'I want to make sure he's OK.'

'Of course he is.'

'After Marcus got in.'

'You're not yourself,' said Mick gently.

'I want to see if Peter's been hurt,' Jamie protested, the probe sharpening.

Mick sighed and then said, 'You be careful then. I'll be standing right beside you.'

'Do you think *I'm* going to hurt him?' Jamie was indignant, conscious of having messed everything up. Marcus had got away – and it was all his fault. He had disappointed Peter. He had made him angry.

Jamie stood over Peter, gazing down at him. Then he saw, or thought he saw, a tiny flicker of movement.

7

Peter's middle finger had definitely moved, Jamie was sure of that as he hurriedly bent over the bed, instinctively locking his own finger around Peter's. There was a slight squeezing movement. Not once, but twice.

'He's coming round.'

'*What?*' Mick bent over Peter too. 'Get off him.'

'His finger. The middle finger squeezed mine.'

'Get off!'

Jamie loosened his grip, and was abruptly pulled away and propelled towards the chair.

'Sit down!' Mick hissed at him.

'No chance. He squeezed my finger. See for yourself, you idiot. Peter's coming out of his coma. Go and look.' Jamie was beside himself with fury. 'Check it out, you big ox.' He was yelling now.

'Don't speak to me like that, and keep your voice down.'

'Why? Don't you want him to wake up? Are you a friend of Marcus's?'

'Who?'

'You're in it together, aren't you? Did *you* give him that white coat? How did you smuggle him in here?'

Mick turned to check Peter again. As he did so, he snapped, 'You're badly mistaken.'

'I'm not,' said Jamie, getting up again.

'Go and sit down.' Mick wheeled round and grabbed his shoulders, forcing Jamie down into the chair and holding him there, while he struggled furiously.

'Get off!' Jamie shouted. 'You're all trying to kill him.'

The door opened and the staff nurse from Bartram Ward came in. She was carrying a hypodermic needle and looked kind but full of authority. Jamie knew he'd lost; he had failed Peter and Marcus was still at large.

'You'll have to hold him,' the staff nurse told Mick. 'But be careful.'

Mick's strong grip tightened.

'Pull up his pyjama sleeve.'

Mick did as he was told, gently but purposefully, and Jamie stopped struggling.

The staff nurse hurriedly swabbed his arm and plunged in the needle. 'You'll feel much better soon,' she told him. 'You need a good rest. You've had a terrible shock, Jamie, and you're all confused.'

'Marcus was here,' he said softly, the drowsiness beginning to steal over him. 'Marcus – got – away –'

'It's going to be all right,' said the staff nurse comfortingly, as Mick relaxed his grip.

All right? Jamie gazed at Peter's bed. Peter wasn't all right. He was in a coma and was being threatened by a killer. He didn't think *that* was all right. It – wasn't – all – right – at –

The ceiling was so low that its blinding, flashing surface reflected continuously in his eyes, making Jamie feel wide awake in his drug-assisted sleep.

From somewhere he could hear the sighing of waves and the mounting whine of a gathering wind. Then the ceiling stopped flashing, turning into a shining screen and Jamie was running flat out towards the edge of the cliff, the pack of boys behind him. Marcus was unmistakable in a tracksuit, but rather than chasing him, rather than egging the boys on, he was standing watching as they all raced towards the clifftop.

Then the flashing began again and Jamie could only see the ceiling of his coffin-like space.

'Well?' asked a distant voice.

'Who is it?' muttered Jamie.

'You'll be saying "Where am I?" next. That's what they say in the movies, don't they?'

'Where am I?' muttered Jamie blearily.

'There you are,' laughed Dad. 'What did I say?'

Jamie surfaced, his head splitting, and as he did so his impossible dreams returned, a painful, menacing memory.

'You're in hospital and getting better by the moment.' Dad sounded unnaturally jolly.

'I've got a headache.'

'Staff Nurse had to knock you out, I gather. Not literally. Gave you a jab, apparently.'

'What for?'

'Don't you remember? You've been out and about half the night. Wandering around the hospital and fetching up in that young man's room. What was his name?'

'Peter.'

Ken Todd gazed uneasily down at his son as if he knew – had known all along – what Peter's name was. What's Dad doing, wondered Jamie.

Trying to test me, to catch me out in some way? He also wondered how much the staff nurse would have told his father. Everything, he guessed, and why not? He must have seemed crazy, although he couldn't remember much of what had happened. Only flashes, like the aluminium ceiling of his coffin-like space.

'I feel lousy, Dad.'

'Would you like a glass of water?'

'No thanks. What's the time?'

'Nine.'

'In the morning?'

Dad pointed at the sunlight streaming through the windows of the ward.

'Come I go home?'

'We'll have to see what the doctor says.'

'I can't stand another night in here,' Jamie said bleakly.

'The nurses might just agree with that.'

'What's that meant to mean?'

'It means that you managed to get into Peter's room twice last night.'

'Did I?'

'You sure did.' Dad seemed to be taking what had happened as some kind of huge joke. Or was that just to cover up his fear?

'What did they say I did?' Jamie began to probe.

'Don't you remember?'

'No,' he snapped.

'The second time you got into Peter's room you were on about the orderly trying to hurt Peter, saying that he'd got away down the corridor. You sounded delirious.'

'Thanks.'

'But of course it's only shock.'

'How do you know that?' asked Jamie sharply. In one way he knew he ought to stay in hospital and protect Peter, and in another he could hardly bear to remain here another minute. The place, like his headache, was really getting to him. But there was something else. A continuous fear. Maybe it would go away if he went home. *And give up?* The phrase stabbed at him painfully. Where had it come from? Of course, Jamie knew exactly where it had come from. Why was he trying to fool himself all the time? Peter was part of him and he was part of Peter. Would *that* be any different when he was away from the hospital?

'While you were out like a light, they took some more tests.'

'And?'

'You came through just fine. No problems at all, and they don't think you had concussion anyway. More like bad shock.'

'So?'

'They'll probably discharge you around tea-time.'

'What about Peter?'

'What about him?'

'I can't just leave him.' But wasn't that exactly what he was going to do? *And give up?* The phrase returned, a shaft of painful light in his head.

'Well –' Dad sounded uncomfortable. 'What can we do?'

'No one knows who he is.'

'They'll soon find out.'

'Can you ask if they have?'

Dad got to his feet with a mock groan. 'I'm getting to be your winged messenger.'

Jamie stared up at his father as if he hadn't heard what he had just said. 'Be quick,' he commanded.

Jamie waited in an agony of apprehension. Suppose something had happened to Peter in the night? He remembered Peter's middle finger squeezing his own. Why wouldn't anyone listen?

Dad returned after what seemed an age, giving nothing away by his determinedly cheerful expression.

'He's had a peaceful night,' he said.

'He would. Did you forget Peter's in a coma?' asked Jamie sarcastically.

'Well, he's not got any worse.'

'Is he coming round?'

'No.'

'But I felt his middle finger move.' Jamie was getting worked up again.

'That's good.' Again the reassuring smile that was so deeply irritating. Why wouldn't Dad take him seriously?

'You don't believe me, do you?' snapped Jamie angrily.

'If that's what you felt –'

They were on the verge of quarrelling and Jamie felt suddenly scared. This hadn't happened in years.

'Why *don't* you believe me?' Jamie's voice was hard and distant.

'Look – I'm as much concerned about Peter as you are. But there's nothing we can do. He's in good hands.' There was an exhausted edge to his father's voice. Then he said hurriedly, 'We can always come back to see him.'

'Can we?' Jamie felt encouraged for the first time.

'You bet. You know I care about him too.'

'Yes.' He sounded doubtful.

'But not as much as you do. You've shared a terrible experience with the guy.'

Jamie was beginning to feel so confused that he didn't even know whether to believe any longer that Marcus had been in Peter's room. Maybe it was a trick of his imagination – a trick brought on by shock. Maybe it was even an hallucination.

'We *can* come in to see Peter soon,' he pleaded.

'Of course.'

'Can I see him before I go?'

'We'll have to get permission –' His father became more hesitant.

'You've *got* to let me see him.'

'I'm sure it can be arranged.' Dad sounded placating again, as if he was afraid Jamie would become hysterical.

*

The doctor was clean-shaven and strong jawed, looking as if he had just stepped out of a TV soap.

'Lousy headache?' he asked.

'Yes.'

'Sorry you had to be sedated, but the shock made you a bit of a – liability round here.'

'I'm sorry.'

'You're very concerned about Peter, aren't you?'

The staff nurse who had accompanied the doctor pursed her lips as if this was a dangerous subject and should be avoided.

Jamie, however, was delighted. The doctor seemed much more open and sympathetic than anyone he had met so far in the hospital.

'Is he coming out of his coma?'

'Not yet.'

'Will he?'

'I don't know. But it would be great if you could go and talk to him before you go.'

'Can I?' Jamie was amazed. Why hadn't anyone else spoken to him like this? He glanced at the staff nurse who looked away.

'You've got a connection. The more you talk to a coma patient the better it is. OK, last night you were scared and mixed up, but if you can calm down you might be helpful.'

'Of course I'll be calm.'

'Just go and talk to him for ten minutes. Say what you've been up to. But there's just one thing –'

'What's that?'

'Be careful. Don't alarm him and don't make any comments that aren't meant to be heard by him.'

'He can hear?'

'We think any coma patient *might* be able to hear.'

'What are his chances?' asked Jamie.

'He's not on a life-support machine and he hasn't got any major brain damage that we can detect. But Peter's had one terrific knock on the head – and the shock to his system was immense. We must do everything we can to stimulate him, despite the fact we don't know who he is or what might interest him.'

'Hasn't anyone come forward?' asked Dad tentatively, clearly in awe of the decisive young doctor.

'Not yet. But it's early days. So why don't you get up, Jamie, and nip down the corridor with your dad? No one's going to drag you back this time, are they, nurse?'

The staff nurse cleared her throat as the doctor winked at Jamie. 'Not if he behaves himself,' she replied grimly.

8

I keep thinking that I'm failing Peter.
I know he needs my help, and I want to
help him, I really do. I just need a sign
that he can hear me. I feel very close
to him...more than close...and I won't
give up on him. I've got to save him
from Marcus...somehow.

As Jamie and his father walked down the
corridors towards Peter's room, Jamie tried to
calm himself down, partly as a result of what the
doctor had said, and partly because he wanted to
try and convince himself that everything had
been in his imagination. Of course it was all
ludicrous, he told himself, and in the dim light of
the hospital corridor he began to successfully
rationalise it all. Whoever had been in Peter's
room last night must have been an orderly who
had a perfectly innocent reason for being there.
And as for the bonding with Peter – or whatever
he should call it – it was ridiculous.

Despite his headache, Jamie slowly began to

feel relieved. Of course some practical worries remained, and the most nagging was Peter's lack of identity. The doctor had said he needed to be talked to, but as Jamie didn't know anything about him what was he expected to talk about?

When they arrived at the nurses' station, Jamie and his father checked in, anxious to know how Peter was getting on.

'No change,' said a nurse who fortunately had not been on duty last night. 'He's still very poorly – and, no, we don't know who he is.' She paused. 'A policeman's been with him and I think he'd like to talk to Jamie before he goes in.'

'Can I sit in on the interview?' asked Ken Todd. 'Jamie's still in a delicate state – and he's a minor –'

'I'm sure you can,' the nurse said reassuringly, leading them both into a small office. 'Do sit down and I'll bring some tea.'

When she had gone, Jamie asked, 'Did you know the police wanted to interview me?'

Dad nodded rather anxiously.

'Why didn't you tell me?'

'It just slipped my mind. Anyway, it's no big deal. Just tell him about the crash and then we'll go in and see Peter. Not for long, mind. We'll need to make a start for home.'

PC Cook was casual and friendly and matter-of-fact, and his attitude made the interview much easier. As they drank the brackish hospital tea, Jamie told him all he remembered.

'Is there anything else?' he asked when Jamie had finished. Jamie thought for a moment, and suddenly his memory seemed to unroll a little more – as if he was stretching out a map and had discovered a folded section he hadn't noticed before. It was an extraordinary sensation and he was more than a little anxious about its origin for his mind no longer seemed to be his own.

'I *think* Peter might have been saying something else, but I can't remember what it was.'

'Not even the ghost of an idea?'

The ghost of an idea? The phrase drummed in Jamie's head. Had he imagined it, or had Peter told him something? Could the shock of the crash have made Jamie forget what he had said? He felt a surge of panic that left him gasping for air.

'What's the matter?' asked PC Cook.

'Just take it easy,' said Dad. 'There's no need to start getting worked up again.'

'There *is* something else,' said Jamie slowly.

'Try and tell me,' said PC Cook, attempting to conceal his impatience.

But Jamie's mind went blank again.

'The train started at Dover?' asked PC Cook.

Jamie nodded.

'So Peter could have got on at any station before Harton. Did he say which one? It would help us to trace his family.'

'No. So what are you going to do?'

'Check out all the schools – particularly boarding schools – in the area between here and Dover who have pupils called Peter and Marcus and maybe someone called Les. That gives us quite a wide field.'

'Shouldn't this school have called round the hospitals already?' asked Dad. 'They must have noticed Peter's missing by now. And if this other kid, Marcus, *is* roaming about –'

Jamie felt a stab of doubt and his fears abruptly returned. 'Wait a minute –'

'Yes?' They were both staring at him eagerly.

'I went to Peter's room twice in the night, and

on both times I thought I saw this orderly searching Peter's clothes. I thought he was Marcus in a white coat.'

PC Cook dismissed the idea immediately. 'An intruder would never have got in. Security's too tight – if he even exists in the first place.'

'Marcus – the orderly – whoever he is – I challenged him – at least I think I did –' Jamie came to a full stop.

'I wouldn't get yourself upset,' said Dad soothingly, trying to calm him down, gazing at PC Cook almost beseechingly who responded immediately.

'I wouldn't get too worked up about what happened last night. You were shocked and probably hallucinating. I'm just going to ring round the schools to be on the safe side,' said PC Cook, getting to his feet. 'You'd better go home now, Jamie, and get some rest. Thanks for all you've tried to remember.' He sounded warm and reassuring.

'I'm not going home,' Jamie rapped out. 'I'm going in to see Peter. The doctor said I should talk to him, that he might be able to hear me, even if he *is* in a coma, and no one's going to stop me.'

'No one's trying to stop you,' said PC Cook, exchanging a glance with Jamie's father. 'I've only got one request though.'

'What's that?'

'Can I come into Peter's room too? I'll sit well away from him.' He sounded humble, as if he had to ask Jamie's permission. Or was that all part of his strategy?

'Why?' Jamie was sullen.

'So I can listen to you talking. That's not going to upset you, is it?'

Jamie shrugged. 'If you want to –'

PC Cook turned to Dad. 'Is that OK by you?'

'I suppose so. But what's the point? Peter's not going to be able to communicate.'

'Jamie just might remember something else, however small. That's a possibility, isn't it?'

Jamie thought it might be.

Directly he stood by the bed, Jamie felt excruciatingly self-conscious.

'I'm going home, Peter,' he said hesitantly. 'I'm feeling better now. But – but I'm not going to desert you. I'll be back as soon as I can.' Then he suddenly forgot Dad and PC Cook sitting in the back of the room as he looked down into the thin, white features. 'Can you hear what I'm saying, Peter? Can you hear me?' Jamie paused. 'If you *can* hear me – raise your middle finger.'

Nothing happened.

'You've got to hear me, Peter. You've got to try and make contact. If you don't – well, you've got to.'

Still nothing happened.

Jamie leant over Peter's bed until he was very near his pale face.

'You've got to listen to me. Can you hear? If you *can* hear, raise your middle finger.'

But Peter's hands remained stiffly spread out on the sheet and there was not a hint of the slightest movement.

Nevertheless, Jamie continued to try for the next few minutes until his headache got worse and frustration overwhelmed him to such an extent that he almost lost his temper.

'Come on,' said Dad. 'We've got to get back now. You're getting exhausted and he's not responding.'

'He's got to.' Jamie was on the verge of tears. 'Let me have another go.'

Ken Todd placed a hand on his son's shoulder but his touch was immediately shrugged away.

'I've got to try again.'

'No.' Dad gripped Jamie's shoulder much more fiercely. 'We're going home now. You'll only upset Peter if you keep pushing like this.'

'Upset him?' demanded Jamie incredulously. 'How can I do that?'

'Don't you remember what the doctor told us. There's every chance of Peter hearing what's being said to him and we should be careful not to —'

'If he can hear,' hissed Jamie, 'then why can't he let me know?'

'Because his mind won't let him. Peter's not ready. Not yet anyhow.'

'I agree,' said PC Cook. 'Come back tomorrow and talk to Peter some more. We can't put too much pressure on him now. It's early days.'

'Don't you want to know who he is?' snapped Jamie.

'Of course I do. But I've no doubt whoever's responsible for him will be calling round the hospitals. It's not going to be long now.'

But suppose no one *is* responsible for Peter, thought Jamie. Except me.

9

Now that I'm home, I really feel that I've let Peter down, that I've run away from the situation. What use am I here? I can't stop Marcus from getting to Peter. And I keep hearing Peter's voice repeating the same phrases: 'Marcus could hurt me. You've got to stop him.' But I don't know what to do... I just want it all to be over.

Jamie had felt very weak ever since he got home, but Dad didn't make a fuss. In fact, he seemed to be doing everything possible to please Jamie, including buying a Chinese takeaway. Jamie loved Oriental food and despite his weakness he was starving. He started with sweet and sour prawns and worked his way on to chow mien and rice and beef in black bean sauce.

Dad put on a southern blues tape while they ate which just happened to be Jamie's favourite music, and he felt almost tearful, relieved to be home and safe.

The train crash and the night at the hospital seemed to merge into one remote and confused memory and for a moment, Jamie felt guilty, aware that Peter's coma suddenly felt remote too. Didn't he care any more?

Then, just as he was finishing off the last of his Chinese feast, he had a dreadful thought. Where was his anorak? Had he left it at the hospital?

Jamie always wore the anorak whenever he could to conceal the fact that he was overweight, much to the derision of his fellow pupils. 'Here comes the anorak,' they would yell in the playground. 'Will you welcome anorak boy!'

'Dad?'

'Yes, Jamie?'

'Where's my anorak?'

'Safely in the hall cupboard.'

'You didn't forget it then?'

'How could I? You never wear anything else.' Dad grinned at him and gave Jamie another large helping.

'I'm spoiling you,' he said. 'Enjoy it while you can.'

But Jamie couldn't get the anorak out of his mind. Now he knew where it was all he could think of was that it had deep pockets. What was the point of that? It was like an unfinished question. Why did he keep thinking about the pockets?

'What would you like to do this afternoon? Have a rest? Take a walk in the park?' asked Dad, breaking in on his thoughts. 'In that order, or any other order you like?'

'In that order,' grinned Jamie, knowing the offer would give him the opportunity to examine his anorak at his leisure. 'Thanks for the takeaway.'

Burning with expectation Jamie said hurriedly, 'I'll just have that rest. Don't let me sleep too long.'

He darted out of the room, running straight to the hall cupboard, where he pulled open the door and dragged out his precious anorak.

Once up in his room, Jamie sat on the bed and began to search the pockets, not knowing why he was doing so. In them he found two half-empty packets of chewing gum, a boiled sweet covered in fluff, a biro without a top, an apple core and half a sugar mouse. He surveyed the objects uneasily. They were truly a disgusting collection. Could there be anything else? A curious compelling instinct drove him on, and he dug his hands back into the pockets.

Suddenly he wrenched his right hand away as if he'd been stung.

Gingerly, he pulled out a grubby envelope, and as he opened it photographs spilled out on to his duvet. He gasped. How had these got into his pocket?

Look after them.

Jamie remained motionless. Had he said the words to himself? Or had they just crept into his mind?

Look after them.

Jamie shivered as he began to sort through the photographs with a shaking hand, trying to work out how they had got into his pocket. He remembered Peter pushing him back into the seat of the train. Could he have shoved the envelope in there without him noticing? Jamie supposed that it might be possible. There were six pictures, all practically identical, showing an elderly man and a teenager with a shock of black curly hair – hair that was instantly recognisable. Jamie felt a thrill of excitement. This was Marcus. So he'd been right about the 'orderly' after all. Jamie felt deeply relieved and then increasingly anxious.

Marcus was standing outside the ground floor window of a large house. An elderly man was inside, handing him a small package. Was this Les? He had a high-domed bald head and an oval face with a small, neatly trimmed moustache.

Jamie knew he had to give the prints to PC Cook for they would not only help to establish Peter's identity but also the circumstances of his running away. He shoved the whole lot back into the envelope and then into the pocket of his anorak as he dragged it on. He would go downstairs straight away and tell Dad what had happened and the responsibility could be shared.

But as he walked to the door, Jamie experienced such a blinding wave of fatigue that he sat back on his bed – and then stretched out, still in his anorak. Jamie was sure that Peter was trying to tell him something, but what? For a few moments he fought against the sleep that was invading him like a marauding army – but it was no use. He was utterly exhausted and *had* to close his eyes, to stop fighting, and forget what he had to do. It felt as though his mind was not his own.

*

He was back in the aluminium room with the shiny ceiling pressed down hard, seeing his reflection gradually become misty and insubstantial again, until he was staring up at Peter.

'Suddenly a command entered Jamie's mind. *Don't.*

Don't what, he wondered, not sure now whether he was asleep or not. He tried to move but failed, and with a conscious effort tried again. Nothing happened. It was as if he was locked into his body, unable to get out, and for a moment Jamie could no longer feel his heart beating. His breathing had stopped and he was utterly terrified, gasping for breath again and again until his lungs started to function once more in a shallow sort of way. Jamie had the impression that he had become a fish-like being, swimming about under the sea, visiting dark caverns, diving deep under fronds of seaweed.

Don't. The word came again as Jamie drifted. *Don't.* The word echoed on the still air, repeating itself over and over again in a measured rhythm. *Don't. Don't. Don't. Don't.*

Jamie was watching a dense, smooth sea that flowed like liquid lead. A beach shook below him and black rock trembled above.

Then he woke to his father's touch. 'What's the matter?' Jamie mumbled, still heavy with sleep.

'Nothing,' said Dad. 'How are you feeling?'

'OK.'

'You asked me to wake you. I'm only obeying instructions.'

Jamie hadn't wanted to be woken. It was as if a dark knowledge was about to be revealed and had then been abruptly withdrawn.

'You're sure you're OK?' Dad was anxious now.

'I'm fine.'

His father stared at him for a moment and then said in a rush, 'Will it be all right if we go in half an hour?'

'Of course it will.'

'I could always go round later.'

'Round where?' said Jamie.

Dad came clean. 'Gran's had a bit of a cold. I thought I'd pop round and see if she's OK – but if you want to go right away –'

This was nothing out of the ordinary. Gran lived nearby and was fiercely independent. Dad often worried about her.

'Go and check her out,' said Jamie at once.

'Shan't be long.' Dad was looking very

worried, as if everything had just got too much for him. Jamie knew the feeling. 'Are you going to be all right on your own for half an hour?'

'Of course I will. Tell Gran something for me.'

'What? What is it?'

'I'm going to go on a diet. I'm going to a gym. I'm going to get myself together.'

Dad bent over the bed and kissed Jamie on the forehead. 'After all you've been through, you shouldn't rush into –'

'I don't want to be a wimp any more.'

'You're *not* a wimp.'

'Or wear an anorak all the time.'

Why wasn't he telling his father about the prints, he wondered. He knew he should, but there was something stopping him. Jamie tried to blurt something out but the words stuck in his throat and wouldn't come out.

'What's the matter?' asked Dad anxiously.

'What do you mean?'

'You look as if you can't catch your breath.'

'I'm fine,' said Jamie firmly. 'Just fine. Go and check on Gran and give her my love.'

10

Every time I try and tell someone about Peter it's as if an invisible force gags me and cuts off my words. Can Peter really be that powerful? And why doesn't he want me to tell anyone about the photos anyway? At least he can't stop me from writing in my diary. And I'm making a note here and now that as soon as Dad gets back, I'm going to show him the photographs and then we can go and see PC Cook. Peter can't stop me...So why am I taking any notice of the word that keeps coming into my head. DON'T. That's all I'm hearing... But give me one good reason why not...

Jamie shut his diary and was about to get off the bed when he noticed the previous page was slightly torn. He felt annoyed. Jamie had a neat and orderly mind and didn't like his possessions being damaged.

Turning back the pages he was suddenly

shocked to see a couple of sentences in sloping handwriting had been crammed in just above the tear and below the last entry.

As he began to read, Jamie felt increasingly uneasy. He couldn't remember writing this.

DON'T even start to think about showing <u>anyone</u> those prints.

Jamie's uneasiness turned to acute anxiety and a bitter chill crawled about his stomach, sharp and painful. This was definitely a warning from Peter. He couldn't keep him out of his mind and now he was even writing instructions in his diary. Jamie didn't know what to do. He needed to keep busy, keep his mind off Peter. His room seemed to have become horribly small, but when he went downstairs and switched on the TV, the picture appeared so large that it was threatening.

Jamie surfed the channels for a while, finally fixing on a nature programme that was showing a huge field of wheat ruffled by a strong wind, waves rippling towards the horizon like an ocean. He watched, almost hypnotised by the rhythmic movement, but when he tried to get up to fetch a drink, he found his willpower had weakened so much he couldn't get off the sofa. *DON'T*, said the voice in his head as he stared transfixed at the waves of wheat.

He had to get outside. But he still couldn't move. It was as if he was pinned to the sofa by an immense force. His breathing became laboured and difficult again, out of his control, and he could feel himself starting to panic. Eventually, with a super human effort, he wrenched himself to his feet and staggered out of the sitting room and into the hall, pulling open the front door, letting in the glorious fresh air of the early October twilight.

With considerable relief, Jamie rushed outside, slamming the door, and hurried down to the garden gate. It was then he realised he had locked himself out and didn't have a key.

At least he was wearing his anorak. He hunched his shoulders against the wind and dug his hands in his pockets. He felt alone and vulnerable, no longer confident as he had been when he had roamed the hospital corridors, intent on finding Peter.

Dad wouldn't be back for at least half an hour – and maybe longer. Should he go for a walk? Maybe take the alley down to the park? But shouldn't he leave a note first in case Dad came back in his absence, discovered he wasn't in the house and began to panic? He felt around in his pockets for a pen, then remembered that he'd emptied his pockets earlier that day. All he had now was the envelope containing the prints.

Jamie checked his watch. He'd just go down to the park anyway; it wouldn't take longer than a quarter of an hour, and at least he wouldn't be standing outside looking like an idiot. Then, glancing up at the sky, he suddenly felt so small, so threatened that he just wanted to hide, but there was no cover.

Abruptly, his feet began to move and he had the unsettling thought that he was being driven away from home and safety, pushed off into a hostile and menacing world by an unseen power.

The narrow alley that led to the park ran between high garden fences and was overhung by trees. When he had been younger, Jamie had always run down as fast as he could, convinced that small demons inhabited the trees, ready to drop on him at any moment.

Now as he hurried along he recalled his childish fears. Darkness was closing in and as the shadows lengthened the deserted alley looked sinister, and Jamie felt a surge of relief as he neared the park. Suddenly, however, another deeper, darker shadow blocked the way, and Jamie's heart hammered as he came to a halt. Warily, he glanced behind him only to see another shadow at the top of the alley, bulky and still. All his instincts had been right. He had been forced into a trap.

11

Jamie stood indecisively, not able to identify who was standing at either end of the alley. Was he going to be mugged? The shadows looked as if they had no faces.

Then the two figures began to move slowly and relentlessly towards him, their steps soft on the leaf-covered tarmac, soft but purposeful, and in a shaft of moonlight Jamie recognised Marcus's dark curly hair and the elderly man in the photographs with the bald pate and trim, pencil-like moustache. Jamie knew it *must* be Les.

He backed up against the fence, praying that some passer-by would come along. But Jamie knew all too well that few people used the alley.

Marcus stopped a few metres away.

'Why don't you just hand them over? Then we'll let you go,' he said quietly.

'Hand what over?'

'You know,' said Marcus. 'You really do know, don't you?'

So far Les hadn't spoken. He just stood there,

looking at the ground, as if the discussion was distasteful to him. Or was he just embarrassed?

Marcus suddenly grabbed at him but Jamie kicked out with a surge of energy, catching him on the knee. Marcus swore and lost his grip, hopping about in pain, then he made another grab at Jamie while Les just stood there, doing nothing, still staring at the ground.

Jamie put his head down and charged into Marcus's stomach. With a strangled grunt Marcus went down and Jamie began to run, amazed at what he had done. He would never have attacked anyone like this. Even to defend himself. He would never have defended himself like this. Normally he wouldn't even know how. But somebody did.

Go for it. The instruction came into his mind unannounced. *Just go for it!*

The park seemed much bigger and emptier than usual, lit by wan moonlight, trees and bushes rustling in a light breeze.

Jamie ran as fast as he could but he knew he wasn't making much progress. In front of him, at a distance of about fifty metres, was the main road, criss-crossed by beams of headlights.

Suddenly he seemed to be running through waves of wheat. But how could that be? The park was flat and the grass was short. Nevertheless, Jamie found himself puffing up a sharp rise, terrified of what might happen, the traffic noise replaced by a familiar sound that he quickly recognised as waves crashing on a rocky beach. He could also feel them pounding in his head, the rise changing into a sharply ascending cliff path that was slightly distorted as if he was climbing through strands of ever-shifting mist.

The sound of the waves became louder and the grass beneath his feet was short and sheep-cropped. Glancing back he saw the path seemed to be rising out of the park itself. Night had gone and he was gasping for air on a bright autumn afternoon, the sky covered in fleecy clouds racing across the face of the sun.

Suddenly Marcus appeared behind him, his face twisted in rage, and Jamie realised he was running up to the top of a cliff where he would surely be trapped yet again. Why didn't he double back to the lower path that he could now dimly make out? He would stand no chance on the clifftop. All he could do was to leap into the sea.

Go for it! The instruction flashed back into

Jamie's mind with such ferocity that he almost came to a halt. *Go for it – you fat wimp.* Was that really Peter's voice in his head?

Desperately, Jamie tried to stop climbing the path and drop down to the lower track, but his feet wouldn't let him. With a will of their own, they were propelling him even faster to the top of the cliff.

When he looked back, Jamie saw that Marcus was gaining on him, and was now only a few metres behind.

With the wind at gale force, Jamie reached the end of his climb, and with a feeling of awesome regret found himself on top of the cliff, gazing down at the jagged rocks and lashing foam below. There was a growling as the water withdrew from the shingle until the eerie sound was drowned out by the crashing of the next wave.

Slowly Jamie turned to face his pursuer, standing stock still, his anorak streaming in the wind, clutching at the envelope in his pocket.

Jamie was standing by the side of a dark road that was full of swirling traffic and criss-crossing headlights. Huge trucks blasted their way past him with hardly a gap between them, and Jamie felt Marcus's hand grab at his shoulder and spin him round on the greasy pavement.

He tore himself free and ran at the traffic.

Buffeted by air currents from the trucks, feeling the hot exhaust of a van, hearing hooting which became a cacophony of violent sound, Jamie darted his way through, somehow keeping on his feet, reaching the opposite pavement by a miracle.

He tried to run on, but was overcome by a heavy weight of exhaustion that seemed to pin him down. Now Marcus was coming after him, weaving through the traffic, ducking and dodging.

'Watch out!' yelled Jamie.

Marcus had almost reached him when a minibus grazed his shoulder, throwing him back into the deadly maelstrom.

Jamie saw Marcus go down, trying to roll clear and then being hit again, this time by a motorbike. He lay twitching and writhing whilst trucks and cars and vans skidded to a halt around him, only just avoiding collisions as he rolled over again and then was still. The three lanes of traffic immediately started to clog, the hooting reaching new heights of furious sound.

As Jamie ran towards Marcus a man leant out from the cab of a truck.

'I'll get an ambulance on my mobile,' he yelled.

A crowd gathered on the pavement, jostling for position, gazing down at Marcus who was flat on his back, blood spreading from under him, his lips working but no sound coming out.

Motorists were switching off their engines, realising something had happened and that the traffic might not move on for some time. Gradually a stillness descended on the tarmac.

Jamie closed his eyes against the horror of it all, only to see himself lying back in a seat, the train lurching. Peter was yelling something at him as the carriage reared up but as Jamie tried to read his lips, a hand grabbed at his shoulder. He lashed out and there was a cry of pain as the inside of the train disappeared and the dual carriageway came back into focus.

'What's up with you?' snapped the truck driver. 'You threw a punch at me.'

'I didn't mean to.'

'You high on something?'

'No,' said Jamie defensively.

'Do you know this kid?'

'I just saw him running.'

'Where were you?' asked the truck driver suspiciously.

Jamie pointed to the pavement behind them.

'You sure you don't know him?'

He shook his head.

'I daren't touch him. He's losing a lot of blood.'

Marcus suddenly groaned and his head twisted from side to side. The dark road surface glistened mockingly and Jamie heard the sound of mewing seagulls.

As Marcus was taken away in an ambulance, Jamie sat on the pavement wrapped in a blanket while a police officer squatted down beside him, notebook at the ready.

'Take it easy, son.'

'I'm OK.'

'You're in shock.'

'I've been that way for some time,' muttered Jamie.

'What did you say?'

'Nothing.'

'Do you know that boy? You told the truck driver you didn't.'

'I lied.'

'Why?'

'I was afraid.'

'What were you doing?'

'Nothing. He was chasing *me*.'

'Why?'

'He wanted something I've got.'

'Something stolen?'

'No.' Jamie continued with his stumbling explanation until, at last, the police officer began to understand.

When Jamie had finished, he began to shake all over despite the warmth of the blanket, and PC Renton said quietly and kindly, 'We need to sort all this out. Why don't I get my colleague to take you home and when I've finished here I'll come and talk to you some more.'

Jamie nodded, checking the pockets of his anorak, making sure the prints were still there. *They're safe*, he told Peter.

When Jamie finally arrived home, Dad was beside himself with worry, wondering where he had been. He became even more anxious when he saw he had arrived with a police officer.

When the officer had gone, Jamie began his explanation all over again as Dad gazed at him in mounting agitation.

'Why didn't you tell me all this before?' he asked.

Jamie shrugged. He didn't really know what to say to anyone – except Peter. Then he thought of a way of satisfying his father and added, 'No one would have believed me, would they? I'd got concussion, remember? Maybe I still have.'

'Are you getting headaches?' asked Dad in growing concern. 'If so, we should get you back to the hospital.'

'I need to go back, but not as a patient.'

'You want to see Peter again?'

'You bet I do.'

'And you've still got those prints?'

Jamie dragged them out of his pocket and put them on the table. Dad shuffled them around and Jamie waited for a reaction. By now the shock waves were receding a little.

'They were caught in the act,' said Jamie in sudden triumph.

'We can't be sure,' said Dad cautiously. 'Things

aren't always what they seem. The camera can lie.'

'What do you mean?' demanded Jamie.

'They could be carrying out a robbery – or they could be doing something completely innocent.'

'Such as?'

Dad didn't reply immediately. 'Suppose this Peter set them up?'

'Don't talk rubbish,' yelled Jamie.

'I'm only trying to see both sides of the story. We don't know any of these people and from what you say Peter seems very unreliable. He might have some mixed motives for taking these photographs, for only showing one side of the story. The side he *wanted* to see. It's just an idea.'

'It's a lousy idea,' muttered Jamie.

He felt despair and a kind of cold anger that didn't seem to quite belong to him. Suppose Dad was right? Suppose Peter had set Marcus up? Suppose Marcus was innocent after all?

The questions rattled round his mind. What was he going to do? Jamie remembered how he had lent Peter money to pay his fare – and how rotten he had been to him in return. *No!* The word came into his mind but somehow Peter's usual authority was no longer there.

'I don't want to be right,' mumbled Dad. 'I'd like to believe in Peter too.'

'I *do* believe in him,' said Jamie miserably.

Suddenly he didn't want to talk about Peter any more. Was that because he was no longer sure? He tried to change the subject.

'How's Gran?' he asked.

'Much better. She sent her love.'

Happy endings for some, he thought, the emptiness building inside him. What about Peter then? Villain or victim? He might never find out.

'After PC Renton's been, can we go straight to the hospital?'

'No chance. You're going to get some rest. I'll take you down there in the morning.'

Jamie knew he had to be content with that, but the emptiness inside him increased. It was as if he had lost someone – and was therefore lost himself.

'Have you caught up with Les?' Jamie asked PC Renton when he finally arrived at the house. He sat on the edge of the sofa with Dad, as if he was on guard.

'No. Not yet.' PC Renton was glancing through the prints, turning them over, one by one. 'So they wanted these back badly enough to try and take them by force and then chase you across a main road. Is that what you're saying?'

'Yes.' Jamie paused. 'It looks as if they were carrying out a burglary, doesn't it?' he asked anxiously.

'They might have been. But we can't question Peter yet.'

'He's still in a coma, I suppose.'

PC Renton shook his head. 'Didn't you know?'

'Know what?' Jamie gazed at PC Renton in confusion.

'The hospital reckon Peter's coming out of that coma. He can move his hands and he's whispering, but no one can make out what he's trying to say.'

12

I can hardly believe everything that's happened. It's 11.00 PM and I'm desperate to go to sleep, but I'm not sleeping until I've written up my diary, just in case I can't remember it all tomorrow. Marcus has been run over, but it wasn't my fault — he shouldn't have chased me. He was so desperate to get his hands on those photos he followed me across the road. But doesn't his desperation prove his guilt? If only I could know that Peter was in the right. I want to believe in him. Badly. But now I'm beginning to wonder if he's the bully. I know how powerful he can be... And that's really scary.

Jamie slept deeply that night. Towards morning, however, he began to dream that he was once again locked into the aluminium room, with the ceiling descending. He was gazing up into Peter's face, watching his mouth form words that he couldn't hear. But rather than feeling a sense of release Jamie was growing increasingly afraid, though he wasn't sure why.

Then he woke abruptly to a new day, a grinding headache and an uneasy feeling of agitated apprehension.

The thumping in Jamie's head slowly subsided as he and Dad had breakfast together.

'When are we going to the hospital?' he asked eagerly.

'When we've done the washing up.'

'Do you think Peter's got parents?'

'I hope so. Funny they haven't turned up though.'

'We've got to find out who he is,' said Jamie.

'Don't get yourself too worked up,' replied Dad anxiously.

'I need to know who he is. I've got to help him –'

'Maybe you can't –'

'I've got to.'

Jamie caught his father looking at him strangely.

'You'd be better off seeing Peter on your own,' Dad said to Jamie when they arrived at the hospital. 'I'll wait outside.'

Suddenly all Jamie's determination, his need to help Peter, seemed to drain away. He didn't want to be alone with him, didn't want to find out what was going on. Suddenly all he wanted was Peter out of his life – and mind – for ever.

But directly Jamie arrived in Peter's room, he felt ashamed, for he still looked incredibly ill and helpless. His face was chalk white and his lips were moving in a continuous whisper.

'It's me.' Jamie sat down by the bed. 'It's me, Jamie.'

But the whispering continued without interruption, as if Peter hadn't noticed Jamie was there. Then he began to listen carefully. Slowly, very slowly, he began to make out what he was saying.

'Won't leave me alone.'

'Who?' asked Jamie. 'Who won't leave you alone?'

But the monotonous drone continued as if he hadn't spoken.

'Who?' repeated Jamie, loudly and firmly.

'Marcus.'

'He bullied you?'

'Marcus.'

'Did he chase you?'

'Marcus.'

'Did he chase you on to the clifftop?'

'Marcus.' It was as if Peter's mind had got stuck in a groove.

'You photographed them stealing something, didn't you?'

'Marcus,' came the monotonous repetition.

'Did you photograph –'

This time the whisper came as an interruption. 'Don't.'

'Don't what?'

'Don't ask.'

'Ask you what?'

There was no reply.

'Did you take a photograph of Marcus and this Les stealing something?'

'Necklace.'

'Stealing a necklace?'

'Necklace.'

'Whose necklace?'

'The wife.'

'Whose wife?'

'Head's wife.'

'How did you know when to take the photographs?'

'Overheard them talking.'

'Where?'

'Behind the gym.'

'Where were you?'

'In the bushes.'

'You were following them?'

'In the bushes.' Peter's voice was getting hoarser and softer, and Jamie knew he had limited time.

'What were they going to do with the necklace?'

'Les knew.'

'Someone who would give them money for the necklace?'

'Give them money.'

'So you took the photographs to prove Marcus and Les were stealing the necklace?'

Peter was silent and Jamie repeated the question.

'So you took the photographs to prove they were stealing the necklace?'

Still Peter didn't reply. Was he getting tired? Several times his eyelids flickered but his eyes stayed closed, his face pale and strained.

'You've got to tell me.' Jamie was insistent. 'I'm your friend.' He paused and then corrected himself. 'I *could* be your friend. You've got to tell me the truth.'

'No way.'

The hoarse words were forced out and Jamie realised that in this final battle of wills they were both on more equal ground. Whilst in his coma, Peter had had to use every inch of his willpower to survive, to break out, to reach him. *Someone's got to help me. How about you?* But how *had* he helped Peter, wondered Jamie. Then he realised that he had cared about him – that Peter had *made* him care. But now that Peter had broken out of his aluminium room and the ceiling was no longer descending, his willpower was exhausted and he couldn't influence Jamie so much. But Jamie knew that he could never rest until he found out what Peter's motives had really been when he took the photographs.

'Was it a set up?'

Peter opened his eyes.

'Were Marcus and Les really stealing the necklace? Or was there another reason for them being there? A perfectly innocent one?'

There was a buzzing sound and Jamie looked up to see all the lighting strips, including the one that had been replaced, glowing very brightly. Then the dazzling intensified and hard, searing light burnt into Jamie's eyes. With considerable effort he tore his gaze away, glancing down at Peter who was staring up at him.

'Who's Les?' asked Jamie weakly, conscious that Peter was still on the winning side.

'School caretaker.' His voice was barely audible.

'Why did you want to get him into trouble?' Jamie took the initiative again.

'I didn't.'

'Did you play tricks on him?'

'Sometimes.'

Jamie's mind was in overdrive. '*Did* you set them up?'

'Deserved it.' Peter closed his eyes against Jamie's persistence.

'Who are you?'

There was no reply.

Jamie changed tack. 'What's the name of the school?'

'St James's. Dover.'

'You're a boarder, aren't you? Where do your parents live?'

'Fostered.'

Jamie gazed at him anxiously, feeling Peter's isolation. 'Who are you?' he repeated.

For a while Peter still didn't reply. Then he spoke so softly that once again Jamie could hardly hear him. 'Peter. Peter Carrington.'

When Jamie finally emerged from Peter's room, Dad asked eagerly, 'What did you get out of him?'

'Not a lot,' he replied. 'Nothing conclusive about the photos. But at least he told me who he is.' For the first time since the accident, Jamie felt as if he had a clear head. Now he had actually admitted who he was, perhaps Peter was no longer imposing his will on him, or had that all been in his imagination anyway?

'The hospital say they know who he is too,' said Dad. 'His foster parents are on their way.'

'What about Marcus?' Jamie asked.

'Fighting for his life,' replied Dad grimly. 'I'm really sorry. You're not to blame yourself.'

But Jamie did blame himself and although he was sure Peter wouldn't have been told about Marcus yet, he hoped he would feel bad too.

After a cup of tea, Dad and Jamie walked slowly down to the hospital reception where a large number of workers in uniform had gathered. Their identification tags gave their names and the fact they worked for an electrical contractor. One of them was putting up a notice on the reception counter.

WE APOLOGISE FOR
THE ELECTRICAL FAULTS
CURRENTLY BEING EXPERIENCED
IN THIS HOSPITAL.
URGENT REPAIR WORK IS NOW
BEING UNDERTAKEN.

Then Jamie saw a familiar face. The man he knew as Les was sitting dejectedly on a seat near the hospital shop, reading a newspaper – or rather holding the pages up in front of him, for as they approached Jamie saw his eyes were glazed over, staring ahead but taking nothing in.

'That's Les,' he whispered to Dad. 'I'd like to talk to him. Why don't you go and sit outside in the car? He won't want to speak to me in a crowd.'

'I don't think we're a crowd,' began Dad, but then he changed his mind. 'Maybe you're right. I'll sit in the coffee shop and keep an eye on you both from there.'

'You're not to come charging over.'

'I'll only do that if you're in trouble,' he promised.

'Les?' asked Jamie tentatively.

Les started and dropped his paper, looking around him uneasily. Fortunately the other seats were empty.

'What do you want?'

'Peter's been talking to me.'

'What about?'

'I can't say.'

'So you've come to wind me up too, have you? I wouldn't bother. I've made my decision. I've come to see Marcus and the Head's on his way up here. I'll talk to him before I go to the police.'

'Peter faked the photos, didn't he?' demanded Jamie. 'That's what you're going to the police about.'

Les didn't reply. He looked down at his hands. 'I'm sorry for chasing you,' he said. 'I was desperate. And now look what's happened to Marcus. They won't let me see him. His parents are up in the ward. Did you know he's slipped into a coma?'

Jamie gazed at Les Barker incredulously. 'Like Peter?' he whispered.

'Just like Peter.'

There was a long silence between them.

'Why did Peter do it?' Jamie asked hesitantly. But did he really want to know? Then he realised that he *had* to know.

Les shrugged. 'It's not his fault. He had a rough time at home with his real parents. His foster parents are decent folk, but they've had a bumpy ride with him too. Peter thinks the world's against him – and he's fighting a constant battle against everyone and everything. I'd had several run-ins with him about his attitude and Marcus was always on to him for hurting his brother. The photographs were the perfect opportunity for him to get back at us.'

'Why did Marcus try and get the prints from Peter? Why didn't he – or you – just go to the Head and explain what had happened?'

'It wasn't as simple as that.'

'Why not?' Jamie demanded.

Les Barker looked away. 'We were guilty,' he said quietly. They weren't faked. And then Peter did a runner, didn't he – with his polaroid.'

'He didn't go to the police.'

Les shrugged. 'Maybe he just wanted to have us in his power – or maybe he was just plain scared. Either way, Marcus and I were as scared as he was - and now look what's happened.'

Les suddenly put his head in his hands.

Jamie gave Dad a wave as he ran back in the direction of Peter's room. Dad yelled at him to come back, but Jamie didn't stop – couldn't stop. If he did, they might stop him from seeing Peter again so soon and he *had* to see him.

But when he arrived, Jamie saw Mick, the muscle-bound orderly, emerging from Peter's room.

'Not you again,' he said.

'I've got to see him.'

'Well – you can't.'

'The doctor said I could.'

'No one told me that.' Mick stood there, looking like an enraged gorilla. 'So push off.'

Just then a loud humming came from the overhead lighting and Mick looked up in alarm. As he did so, all the strips down the corridor exploded in a shower of plastic.

'You stay there,' yelled Mick as he charged away in the direction of the nurses' station.

Hurriedly, Jamie took the chance he was sure Peter had given him.

Moments later he was standing by Peter's bed, looking down. Peter's eyes were open now.

'You're in the clear,' Jamie whispered. 'You were telling the truth.'

'What's that to you?' whispered Peter, now much more his old self.

'You didn't set them up. Les has confessed.'

'They're a couple – of – crooks.'

Jamie said nothing, gazing down into Peter's eyes. Then he asked softly, 'What were you going to do with the photos?'

'Give them to the police.'

'Why did you give them to me?'

'Safe-keeping.' Peter closed his eyes again. Was this fatigue? Or evasion?

'You weren't going to blackmail them, were you? From a distance?'

For the first time since he had come out of the coma, a guilty grin appeared on Peter's pale face.

13

A week has passed and I'm beginning to feel normal again. When I look back at last weekend, it seems that Peter knew more in his coma than any of us knew in life — perhaps he'd reached some near-death experience that gave him special knowledge...what a spooky thought! Anyway, I'm off to visit him in a minute — we went through a lot together and I still feel very close to him — I really hope we can be friends.

Jamie watched Peter leaning over Marcus's bed. Marcus lay curled up, one hand cupping his chin and the other bunched into a tight fist. His eyes were tight shut. Marcus had so far showed no sign of coming out of his coma.

Peter's stare intensified and Jamie's head ached as he felt the strength of that willpower, this time thankfully not directed at him.

Peter gazed down at Marcus without wavering and Jamie glimpsed the aluminium space with the descending ceiling reflecting blinding white light. He glanced at Marcus again and felt shock waves run through him. Could his left eyelid be flickering? Was his hand uncurling a fraction?

14

Marcus Witley, a fifteen-year-old pupil of St James School, Dover, has slowly begun to emerge from a coma. He had been unconscious for over a week after a road accident. By a bizarre coincidence, in an unrelated incident, another pupil of the school, Peter Carrington, is also recovering from a coma at Harton County Hospital.

Doctor David Blake commented, 'Our new state-of-the-art laser technique has been successful in both cases and will be used again on other coma patients.' He went on to explain—

Jamie slowly put the paper down. What Dr Blake didn't mention was that Peter had sat by Marcus's bedside all that week, gazing down at him. Focusing his will...

Jamie glanced up at Dad. 'Have you read this?'

He nodded.

'What do you reckon?'
'I think Dr Blake made a breakthrough.'

Saturday, 23rd

We'll have to see about Dr Blake's breakthrough. What will happen to the next patient in a coma if Peter isn't there to make contact with them? Or does the laser treatment really work? I think meeting Peter has done me a lot of good. I don't feel like a wimp in an anorak any more. I feel more confident, stronger in my own mind. I reckon Peter gave me that. Peter's back at school now and Dad and I are going to visit him tomorrow. I wanted to go at first, but now I'm really nervous about seeing Peter. I'm worried about his willpower. I hope he won't use it on me. Not again. I'm afraid of what will happen if he does.